SAVAGE DELIGHTS

TWO DARK TALES

CANDACE ROBINSON

For those who wanted a savage delight … or
preferably two

The embracing skeletons of two lovers were once discovered, and in her hand, the woman held a notebook with these two tales.

TALE
ONE

A BIRTHDAY HEX

Gleaming against the bright sun, a long strip of black cloth rested in Nana's palm. Charm arched a brow at it while she clasped her boyfriend's hand.

It was Charm's eighteenth birthday today, and as a surprise, her family had come to pick her up at her shared apartment with Sage.

"Come on, Sage, stop clinging to Charm and wrap the blindfold around her eyes," her mom—Jade—singsonged, lightly smacking their hands apart.

"Don't worry," Nana said, hugging Sage first, then handing him the dark fabric. "We'll return Charm in time so you can have a birthday dinner with her."

"Take your time." Sage smiled, giving Jade a goodbye hug next. When he turned to Charm, his hazel irises were sparkling, his grin growing wider. "Assume the position."

Charm rolled her eyes but faced away from him as Sage's soft fingertips grazed her cheeks, his touch igniting butterflies in her stomach as they always did. She'd moved in with Sage at the end of their senior year, leaving behind their families' expensive houses to have their own space. They'd now been living together for two months in a rinky-dink apartment, working awful jobs for the time being, her at an ice cream parlor, him at a grocery store. But with Sage, it was worth every damn cockroach.

Darkness enveloped Charm as Sage tightened the fabric, not a single speck of light slithering in.

It was suffocating.

"Do we really need this forsaken thing?" Charm complained, tugging at the silky material of the blindfold.

"Yes, you have to wait for the *birthday* surprise," her mom said in that singsong voice that was starting to grate on Charm.

"It's your lucky day," Nana added. "And there will be no purse or phone, just you."

"Fine," Charm grumbled. With her eyes covered, it would feel like an eternity, but she would keep those exaggerated thoughts to herself since her family was trying to do something nice for her.

"It'll beat my *fun* day at work. Have a good time, and I love you," Sage whispered, pressing his soft lips to hers, his cypress scent caressing her nose.

"I love you," Charm murmured back, wishing she could see his face.

"Come on," Jade purred. Charm could tell her

mom was grinning as she took her arm and drew her away from Sage. Nana grasped Charm's other arm and together they guided her into the backseat of the car.

Jade started the car and took off a little too fast, Charm's head hitting the seat. Charm wondered where she was being taken—she'd never had a "surprise" like this from her mom or Nana, but she was hoping it would be somewhere she hadn't been before. Maybe a secluded park near the historical buildings in Houston or Galveston?

Time seemed to go on and on when she finally asked, "How much longer?"

"It's only been thirty minutes, my impatient grandchild, but you must have ESP because we're here," Nana said, laughing while removing Charm's blindfold.

The world was a blur—one big blob of mixed colors. Charm blinked until everything came into focus. A wide smile crossed Nana's cheeks as she peered around the passenger seat at her. Jade glanced back at her too, with a smile mirroring Nana's, before returning her attention to…

They weren't on a road anymore. Trees surrounded them. Jade had driven off the road and they were now buried inside a forest with no sign of pavement anywhere. A whole forest of ash trees, ones Charm had only seen in books. Her lips parted as she gazed at their wide forms, the moss dangling from gnarled branches, holes that led deep into their trunks.

Jade finally slowed to a stop in front of the largest ash tree, its crooked branches curving in all directions. Thick green vines hung from its limbs, obscuring what lay beyond. The tree looked like something out of a horror movie, one where it secretly ate babies or some shit.

What were they doing here?

"Come on," Jade said before opening the car door at the same time Nana did.

Charm unbuckled and stepped out of the vehicle. Her lips parted as the breeze rumpled her short blue hair. She brushed her bangs from her brows, then studied the trees. Their dark green leaves rustled and their branches creaked in the wind. "What is this?" Her heart pounded as the trees seemed to breathe in sync with her, their leaves inhaling and exhaling, their soft noises like whispers.

She's here. It's time, they appeared to say.

Charm shook her head, pushing what had to be only her imagination away. There was no way the trees could be talking.

Her long, blonde hair billowing behind her, Jade waved a hand at the giant ash tree. The thick green vines on the tree's right side lifted, revealing an ivory boulder, freckled with small craters, that was almost as tall as her mom.

Charm's eyes widened, her heartbeat rocketing.

What the hell?

Jade placed a palm on her shoulder, the same hand that had made the vines *move*. "Don't be afraid," she said gently, her deep brown eyes— matching Charm's—holding her gaze steady. "It's your eighteenth birthday, and you come into your magic today."

Charm's breath hitched as she peered at the faces of her mom and Nana. *Magic?* It couldn't be true, but then she'd just seen her mom move vines without even touching them, could still hear the odd whispers of the forest. Her fingers itched to call Sage before she remembered she was told to leave her phone back at the apartment.

"What do you mean?" Charm frowned. "Where are we?"

"We'll explain everything once we're inside." Nana pointed to the boulder, then drew her dark braid, peppered with white streaks, over her shoulder.

Inside a rock? As if answering Charm's internal question, Nana swiped her hand to the side and a door creaked open in the center of the boulder. The stone had been smooth, devoid of even a single crack, only moments before. For a split second, Charm wanted to run, but these weren't strangers. It was her mom, her nana, and they'd been there her whole life. They'd raised her together since Charm's dad had died before she was born. She trusted them.

Charm took a deep swallow and nodded.

Jade motioned for her to follow, and Charm padded behind her through the thick grass with Nana hovering closely.

"It looks dark in there." Charm squinted at the door in the boulder. "Do you have a light?"

Jade waved her hand once more, and a weak, pale light shone from inside the boulder. Charm licked her lips and arched a brow when they ducked through the door. A pleasant, spicy-sweet aroma filled the air as Charm descended a dark stone staircase behind her mom. It was a familiar scent from her family's home. The aroma made her dizzy, filling her with lightness and expectation.

Hundreds of tiny white bulbs shone within the narrow space. Fairy lights? Beneath the warm glow, ivory brick walls led them deeper into the earth. This was … weird. Charm was desperate for her phone now, wanting to look up anything involving magic. Demons? Faeries? Witches? Angels? She'd always believed a higher power was out there, but whatever her mom and Nana's role was in this, she would soon find out.

Charm wished Sage was here, to see what she was seeing. They'd been together since the ninth grade, and he wasn't just her boyfriend but her best friend. He was sweet and funny as hell. While most high school relationships didn't last, Charm had always known he was the one. Knew it from the moment she saw him. If she hadn't experienced it for herself, she never would've believed in love at first sight, and she would've been the first to say it was bullshit. But it wasn't. Had it possibly been some kind of intuition?

At the bottom of the stairs stood a pristine ivory archway with towering pillars on either side. Obsidian beads hung from the center, forming a curtain. As she drew closer, through the eerie light, Charm could see the pillars weren't smooth but covered in small carvings. Naked men's bodies, twisted and stitched together into a macabre pattern, ran up and down the ivory. She frowned at the sinister art, not finding a single female form among the engravings. The men appeared to be screaming, their faces grimacing in pain. *Strange.*

A swishing sound caught Charm's attention as Jade pushed the beads aside. Jade gestured them through, and Charm inhaled sharply while peering around the wide-open space that would make a decent-sized living room. Deer and ram skulls lined the black walls, and every other inch of the area was marked in white chalk with drawings and numbers she didn't understand. Ruby-colored chandeliers hung from the ceiling in a circle, casting their glow across the space, highlighting a massive round table beneath them. Charm counted twenty chairs surrounding it, all with black cloaks draped over their backs. On the table, in front of each chair, rested a silver goblet and a single white candle. At the center of the table sat a small cauldron.

Charm's heart struck her rib cage, nervous at what was happening. She wasn't sure if her family was going to try to do some sort of séance, but she wouldn't join in on summoning any damn demons. A part of her still didn't believe this was actually happening. But the strange, sweet smell of this place and the presence of her family assured her she wasn't dreaming.

"You need to tell me what's going on." Charm folded her arms, her fingers digging into her skin. "Are you trying to conjure the devil or something?"

Jade cocked her head and let out a high-pitched laugh. "We don't need a man to do what we do. We answer to nature. We are each our own witch."

Witch.

Charm sighed in relief. Nature. Nature was a good answer. Good witches then. She could deal with that.

Jade set her purse on the table and opened it to fish out a silver necklace. A purple amulet dangled at the end of the chain, the light from the chandeliers bouncing off the jewel.

"This will ignite your magic for now"—Jade held up the necklace as she moved to stand in front of Charm—"but after tonight, when everything is finished, you won't need its help."

"After what's finished?" Charm wrinkled her

nose.

Jade ignored the question and unclasped the necklace. Charm glanced at Nana, trying to get an answer from her, but she stayed silent too. Something was wrong. The sweet aroma of the place turned rotten.

Charm went to take a step back, yet Jade was quicker, clasping the piece of jewelery around her neck.

As soon as the amulet brushed Charm's collarbone, her heart pumped fast, too fast, while something—a wholly new sensation—coursed through her veins. A caress at first, building and building. Charm's lungs could barely keep up with the adrenaline flowing through her. It wasn't pain, but *something* else. Panicked, she clawed at her throat, trying to rip the necklace off, yet it wouldn't budge. She choked as the words escaped her mouth. "What did you *do?*"

"Relax." Jade cradled Charm's face in her hands. "Breathe. This amulet holds the essence of the first witch—it is ancient, its power raw. It takes a moment to get used to the magic."

And then, as though to prove what Jade had said wasn't a lie, the rush inside Charm dulled to a soft thrum. She drank in breath after breath until each one came out steady.

Jade released Charm's face. "You've been taking care of yourself for a long time now. By age, you may be a woman, but you've been one for a while. However, tonight, you will access your birthright and become a witch. The rest of the coven is on its way and you will bring us the refreshment at 10 p.m. sharp."

This … this was really happening. It wasn't something Charm would wake up from. She studied her family. There were never any hints that either one had magic, could do things most people believed didn't exist. But as the energy hummed within her, raw and new, it felt right. She'd seen plenty of movies about magic. Hell, she remembered *The Craft* most clearly. Her mom had always laughed at parts that Charm had never found funny. And as she looked back over the years, maybe there *were* signs that Jade had held secrets. Charm's family, these two women she loved and admired, sometimes smelled just like the inside of this boulder, but when Charm would ask them about it, they'd blame it on incense. Yet Charm had never seen any incense sticks around her old house. How could they have lied to her about this?

Oblivious to Charm's anxious thoughts, Nana clapped her hands together and said, "Now, before you return tonight, we'll drop you back at home and you'll couple with Sage, then reap his life."

Charm's head jerked up and she stilled. *Holy hell.* Had she heard Nana correctly? No, she must not have.

"Excuse me?" she rasped, blinking hard. The amulet pulsed against her flesh. "What did you say?"

"Sage is a good boy, but he'll need to die today." Nana's eyes held no pity, only something that Charm interpreted as … encouragement. "We know you have a fondness for him. We all did for ours, but you will understand once he's gone. Once true power courses through your veins."

Nana's words rang in Charm's ears, *screaming*, the sound nearly causing her pain.

"What do you mean? What have *you done*?" Charm's hands flew to her mouth, shaking. She hoped what her family was about to say wasn't what she was thinking. But her hope shriveled as both women stared at her in a way that made her blood run cold. They felt like strangers to her. Worse— they felt *dangerous*.

Jade wrapped an arm around Charm's shoulders, and it was too heavy as she spoke, "Your father, your grandfather, your great-grandfather, and so on. They've all had to die for the magic of the coven to stay strong, especially when new daughters are conceived."

Charm ripped away from her mom and backed up into the wall, her hands trembling. "You, you killed—"

"We had to," Jade said, not an ounce of regret shining in her eyes. "Our coven weakening or them dying. It's not really a choice."

Screw the coven.

The morbid images carved into the columns made sense now. Charm winced at the memory of the faces twisted in agony. Was her dad portrayed there too, included among the sacrifices? Her grandpa? Charm had never met either of them, but she'd wanted to, had always wondered what her life would've been like if her dad was there. She thought about Sage then, and about his father—one of the nicest people Charm knew. He took her to art museums and taught her to play chess.

Her mom and Nana had made life good for her, doted on her, but … was all of it a lie?

Lies behind smiles.

Nana crossed her arms and moved toward her, same as she used to when Charm was a child and not paying attention. "You will have sex with Sage when he comes home, get his seed inside you—the amulet's magic will ensure you conceive and that it will be a daughter. Just as all the members of our coven have done over the centuries."

Centuries?

Charm took a deep swallow, thinking again about the men engraved in the archway. So many sacrifices. All she could focus on was how her mom had killed her dad, and how her grandpa had died by Nana's hand. "Then what?" Charm asked, wondering what they'd done after killing a man they loved.

"Then, you will gather his blood into the cauldron and mix in rosemary, mint, and three drops of your blood for the coven to drink tonight."

Her stomach sank and nausea bubbled up her throat. "Why does it have to be him?" Charm asked, her voice shaking. "And why does he have to die?"

"It has to be your true love."

"Maybe he isn't," Charm lied. But she knew. Knew it with her whole damn heart that he was. Knew it from the second she'd walked into that ninth-grade classroom and looked at him. Sage with his curly black hair, his vivid hazel eyes, the dimples in his cheeks, his love for awful movies, the way he ran his hands through her short hair, the way he told her he loved her.

"He is." Nana rotated her shoulders, her expression hardening. "Why do you think we moved here? To have you two meet and naturally fall in love."

Charm's heart pounded. They'd *known*… That was why they hadn't argued when she'd wanted to move in with Sage. It wasn't a coincidence they'd come to Texas. This place had been specifically chosen so she could meet Sage and one day kill him. Her true love. All so that some coven she hadn't known about before today could become stronger.

"Now, this is important." Jade straightened, her voice stern like a command. "Will you do this and take the cauldron?"

"And what if I won't?" Charm challenged.

"Then the coven will step in," Jade said. "One way or another, Sage will die."

Charm's heart clenched. "I understand." She didn't say another word as the cauldron was placed in her hands. It didn't weigh much, but in that moment, it felt heavier than anything she'd ever held.

"Perfect." Happy tears beaded at Jade's lashes as she smiled. "I'm so proud of you."

Charm struggled to breathe, but the amulet, pressed against her neck, seemed to inhale and exhale, just like the trees outside.

"Once this is done," Nana said, "we will leave here and make a home somewhere else. We will prepare for your daughter's arrival, and when the time comes, we will locate her true love before moving once more."

The magic pulsed underneath Charm's skin, the amulet busy at work. "Yes." She wanted to scream no, but she needed to get out of there, get home—away from *them*—and think of a way out of this.

Jade circled her arm around Charm's waist, her grip too tight. "If you don't follow through," she said, her sunny smile at odds with her words, "there will be, shall we say, repercussions."

"Repercussions?" Charm asked, biting her lip.

"You see, Charm," Jade continued, her fingers playing lightly over Charm's collarbone as she lifted the pendant. "This amulet, it can be your friend today. Or it can be your enemy."

Nana cocked her head. "You don't want it to be your enemy, sweetie."

Charm nodded, but really, all she wanted was to go back to this morning, to before she'd come here. She just needed to get home.

Get home to Sage.

She wouldn't do it—wouldn't kill him. Anger boiled through her as she studied her mom and Nana, their faces serene. Charm had to force herself to look at them and smile.

Neither of them had ever had another man in their lives since murdering their true loves. Charm had been conceived *specifically* for their magic to one day grow stronger. She swallowed her disgust.

"Once you do what is asked of you, proving your loyalty to the coven, you will understand why we do this," Jade said, as if she could sense Charm's thoughts. "You will see that there is no other way. And once you come into your magic tonight, feel this incredible power within you, you will know that its cost is more than justified."

Charm could barely register her mom's words.

I won't kill Sage. I won't kill Sage. I won't kill Sage. I won't kill Sage.

The amulet heated against her flesh, its warmth penetrating straight to her heart.

I will kill Sage.

Charm remained quiet as Jade started the car, the trees' breaths loud in her ears, even with the windows rolled up. She peered out the glass while Jade drove through the foliage, the sun still bright in the sky.

As the car traversed the forest, the trees' branches peeled back. Charm gasped, her eyes widening.

"The trees protect us." Nana pointed out the window. "No matter where we live."

The amulet heated against Charm's chest once more—its warmth lingered on the entire ride back. She could feel its magic not only on her skin, but below it, massaging her muscles, swimming in her blood, and seeping into her bones until it could go no further.

Biting the inside of her cheek, she brushed her fingers against the amulet.

"The magic feels unusual at first," Nana said, leaning around her seat. "But once it's all done and you give into the power, you won't want to take any of it back. Sage will feel like a distant memory after he serves his purpose. We can use our magic to get what we want—wealth, careers, fame—*anything*. It's been that way since the first witch, long ago in Ireland, made a pact with a dark fae who gave her the amulet. It is a great honor to join our coven, and a great responsibility, too."

Charm could see how the power might be tempting, but for the first time in her life, she hated her nana, hated her mom. She stayed silent, gripping the cauldron in her lap until they pulled into the parking lot of Charm's run-down apartment complex.

"I'll see you tonight," Charm said, forcing a smile as she stepped out of the car. She clenched the cauldron even tighter, her nails scraping against the metal.

"I know how you're feeling right now, but after this, you'll count down the days until the moment you give this gift to your own daughter." Jade gave her a reassuring smile.

A gift? To force her daughter to murder her true love? Was that what Charm's life would revolve around? Lying? Manipulating? Betraying? Being in denial? Was it worth the power she was promised?

"One more gift from us." Nana opened the glove compartment and drew out a blue box with a white bow on top, then handed it out the window to Charm.

"Thank you." Charm managed to keep her voice even while placing the box inside the cauldron. She kept her walk steady, casual, as she headed up the metal stairs to her apartment.

Something dark jumped in front of her and hissed, baring its teeth. Charm groaned at the feral cat that hung around her building. "Hello, Diablo." She attempted to scoot the black cat out of the way, but it let out a low, wicked sound before darting off.

"Maybe not hiss at me next time!" she yelled at its mangy back.

Once inside her apartment, she leaned against the door with a sigh of relief. Sage wasn't home yet, but he would be soon.

Charm set the cauldron with her unopened gift beneath the table in the cramped kitchen. She would get this amulet away from her, even if she had to cut off her own head to do it. Whatever would prevent her from killing Sage.

But no matter how hard she dug her fingers into the clasp, it wouldn't budge. The chain wasn't long enough to tear over her head either. Charm growled in frustration as she marched to one of the kitchen drawers and yanked it open. She grabbed a pair of scissors and brought their blades to the necklace, hoping to break the chain. But when she squeezed as hard as she could against the metal, it didn't give way. "Dammit." She hurled the scissors across the room.

Charm needed a plan—she would run. No, she couldn't do that because the coven would still kill Sage. She would tell him to run then, to a place where he couldn't be found. Clenching her jaw, she reached for her phone on the counter. The amulet heated and her fingers stilled against the phone. She wanted to scream, only no sound came out. The amulet knew everything—it could see right inside her head. She would go to Sage's work then, but just before she got to the door, her feet froze in place, her hand unable to reach the knob as she swiped through the air.

"What the hell?" Charm took a step back, gripping her hair as she went into the living room and dropped onto the futon. "I *am* hexed…"

She studied her desk, her open laptop, the TV, the framed movie posters hanging on the walls, her and Sage's shared bookcase filled with more movie memorabilia.

Frustrated, she pushed up from the futon and took the gift out of the cauldron, then headed into the bedroom. If she was a witch, even if she was still uninitiated, there had to be a way to break the hex. *Maybe there's an answer in this gift*, she thought while removing the lid from the box.

A gasp escaped her as her gaze fell to what rested inside—a jeweled silver dagger. Her mom and Nana had given this to her … to use on Sage. A weapon to murder him. Another invisible blade to her chest, a betrayal that kept growing.

She froze when she heard the sound of a key sliding into the top lock. Sage was back early from his stocking job at the grocery store. Realizing she still gripped the dagger in her hand, she darted into the bedroom and shoved it into the nightstand drawer.

As the front door opened, every memory of Sage rushed through her at once. The amulet ignited, warming her skin, becoming hotter. Every inch of her was *burning* with desire.

Charm remembered seeing Sage on her first day at the new school. Liking how his dark curly hair had hung past his shoulders. The way she had talked to him first. How his cheeks pinkened when she'd sat beside him at lunch. She'd made the first move with everything, but not with their first kiss, and not when he'd unbuttoned her jeans, which led to her wanting to touch him too. Her memories continued, moving to their first time together during eleventh grade. Every time they'd had sex, they'd always been careful, used protection.

Rustling came from the kitchen, and the thrum in her veins grew stronger. Her magic was conquering, taking root. This was the amulet's doing. It knew Sage was there—and it wanted Charm to…

She could sense the amulet's appetite, its thirst for power. It had an agency, a will of its own. It wanted and it craved.

Sage's footsteps padded toward the bedroom, toward *her.* The desire within her pulsed harder than her heart as she took a seat on the edge of the bed.

He stopped as soon as his gaze met hers, a playful smile spreading on his face, his dimples showing. "You're back earlier than I thought. I was hoping to have a fancy meal ready for you." His feet were bare, and he had on his dark work pants and white shirt, his hair pulled back into a low ponytail.

"That can wait." She fought against the amulet, trying to conjure the right words. "I need to tell you something. Come here."

Sage furrowed his brow and stepped toward her. "What is it? Are you all right? You're looking a little pale." He came up to her in three long strides and lifted her chin as he sat beside her.

Charm opened her mouth to speak, to tell him everything, but the amulet wouldn't let her.

"Did the surprise not go well?" he asked, studying her face.

It didn't. Not at all. The words rested on the tip of her tongue yet wouldn't spill from her lips. "I'll tell you about it later, but it was … unexpected," she finally forced out. Nothing else would come.

He drew her close. "I know they meant well. They always do." Before today, she would've agreed.

"I love you." She crawled into his lap, straddling his thighs. Blowing out a breath, she wrapped her arms around his neck and rested her head on his shoulder.

"I love you too."

"Remember that one time you snuck into my room," she whispered into the crook of his neck.

"You mean after our first date when I was too damn scared to kiss you?" He chuckled.

"Yeah."

"What about the night you snuck into my room?" She could hear the smile in his voice.

"When I came over to make love to you for the first time but your mom walked in?"

"Yeah."

"That was the worst." Thankfully his mom hadn't brought up *that* matter ever again.

He lifted her face once more, so that her gaze locked onto his beautiful hazel eyes. "It was perfect though. You know why?"

"Why?" she asked softly, her heart beating faster.

"Because it led us to a better first time."

Charm thought about that night, how they'd visited an old cemetery so she could take pictures for class, then they'd walked through the woods and found an abandoned building that had once been a drive-thru theatre. They'd picnicked there before driving to the beach and setting up a tent. She'd lied to her mom, told her she was staying with a friend, and Sage had done the same. Charm was pretty sure now that her mom had known the whole time and had probably been giddy about it. Dread rolled through her.

But an idea formed.

Maybe … maybe she could distract the amulet. Maybe if she appeased it by following through with this first part, the easy part, she could gain herself more time to think of a way out of the second half.

The murder.

She kissed the side of Sage's neck, making him shiver. His fingers dug into her hips as she skimmed the tip of her nose slowly up his throat, then trailed open-mouthed kisses across his jaw.

Charm knew she was being awful by not telling him the truth, but she *couldn't*. She was being a monster, a *witch*, by kissing him now. But if she didn't, the amulet would force her, and she would rather make love to him with her free will. Because this … this she could easily do.

"Dammit, this may sound stupid as hell," he whispered, his fingers tracing soothing circles on her back. "But each day I love you more."

"Then I guess we're both stupid as hell," she murmured, tears pricking her eyes as she cupped his face and placed a soft kiss on his mouth. "I want to be with you in a way I haven't before. Nothing between us."

His chest heaved, and he leaned his forehead on hers. "I want that too. If you're sure."

Charm nodded and crashed her mouth to his, her hands entangling in his hair as if she didn't want to let him ever go, didn't want his life to ever end. He skated his fingers down the valley between her breasts, his touch heating her entire being. The edges of his lips tilted up as he grasped the hem of her shirt before lifting it over her head. With each kiss, another layer of clothing came off, until only skin kissed skin, his hardness against her softness.

God, she was never going to get enough of him. When at last he slid inside her, she moaned, arching her back, the feel of him addictive as ever. They moved in sync, in utter perfection, until he brought her over the edge. The deep, pleasurable magic he always stirred within her, drowning and floating all at once, stormed through her at the same time he groaned, just as true lovers would.

Once they caught their breaths, Charm wrapped her arms around him, tighter than she ever had before. Squeezing her eyes shut, she ignored the amulet's growing warmth against her collarbone. But then the heat became stronger, tugging at her, making her eyes flutter. Hot tears streamed down her cheeks, and she trembled, clenching her jaw as the pain grew sharper.

The amulet was telling her what she must do next. Open the drawer of her nightstand where her jeweled dagger rested. Remove the blade and plunge it into his heart. It would be so simple. Over in mere moments. Sage would hardly feel any pain.

Please, no. Please. Please. Please! There had to be a way out of this nightmare.

There had to be.

But even as she pleaded, even as she begged, fighting with everything her heart held for Sage, Charm leaned over and her hand reached for the drawer instead.

The cauldron's lid rattled in the passenger car seat beside Charm as tears beaded her lashes. She pressed her hand against the lid to stop the sound, which reminded her of what was in the cauldron. With a deep breath, she removed her palm and turned up the radio, letting the heavy drums and guitars fill her ears while she gripped the steering wheel. Sobs threatened to choke her once again, but she was determined to focus on the road in front of her. She must think *only* of the future, of the *only* path left to her. She'd been left with no choice. The amulet purred against her chest, content and sated.

Charm had been driving for almost thirty minutes, and now she was looking for the spot in the forest where her family had taken her earlier. No luck yet. Not a single car's headlights had passed her down the darkened road. She wondered if the coven had placed some sort of spell on this area to keep people away.

Her phone dinged, but she didn't bother to check it. She didn't need any distractions.

Charm flicked on the high beams and squinted, knowing she was getting close.

To the right, something shifted in the darkness as she slowed. She rolled down her window, and the branches stirred, beckoning her. The limbs unfurled, creating a gateway. Heart pounding, she drove carefully over the grass, the car jostling side to side.

The sound of breathing filled her ears once more—the trees inhaling and exhaling. A humming that hadn't been there earlier drifted through the air. Charm listened closely, and it sounded like women singing.

Owls hooted and other birds screeched in the tops of the trees beneath the moon's silvery light.

Up ahead, rows of cars gleamed in Charm's headlights. She spotted her mom's white SUV, but didn't recognize any of the other vehicles.

Charm pulled to a stop, then unbuckled the cauldron and lifted it before stepping out of the car. She bit the inside of her cheek to keep from falling to pieces.

The trees' breaths came to a halt, as though they were listening, waiting for her to speak to them.

"You're right on time," her mom called.

Charm whirled around to find Jade hovering at the boulder's open door, a lantern in her hand. Jade's blonde hair spilled down her chest over a dark hooded cloak.

Holding the cauldron tightly, Charm walked toward the light.

"You got the blood." Jade sighed, greedily taking the cauldron from Charm's hands. "With Sage's death, you're free now. No longer bound to someone who you may not have given a second glance to otherwise."

That wasn't true. She'd never felt chained to Sage. Charm's chest tightened and she pushed down the emotions brewing to the surface. However, she couldn't shove them all away, and her hands clenched at her sides. The amulet purred once more, and she ignored it. "How long did you mourn Dad?"

"After that night, I didn't. I only focused on my freedom, the magic, the future of the coven. Tomorrow, what is left of your sadness will evaporate."

One day? That was it? How? How could Charm be expected to move on from Sage so quickly after murdering him? How could her mom have done that to Charm's dad? How could Nana? And all these other witches who she hadn't even met yet? Would any power in the world justify murder?

Charm held her tongue and followed her mom down the staircase. The fairy lights on the walls guided their way as the spicy-sweet scent enveloped her. The smell of magic, of pulsing power. A smell she had come to despise.

Humming echoed up the stairs from the room below, but Charm couldn't see anything past the beaded curtain except for slivers of light. Her eyes widened at the archway and ivory pillars, now covered in blood that spilled out from the chests of the engraved men.

Jade drew back the beads, a clinking noise echoing, revealing the table in the center of the room that was filled except for two chairs.

The witches' heads turned in Charm's direction, eyes blazing, their smiles welcoming her to their murderous coven. Out of everyone there, Charm appeared to be the youngest. Closest to her in age was a girl with dark braids twisted around her head. The oldest witch was maybe somewhere in her nineties—age spots dotted her temples and hands, and deep wrinkles covered her face. As for the rest of them, these witches were a diverse crowd, all ages, all sizes, all skin colors. All having murdered their true love while seeming to not give a damn.

They stood from their seats, smiling with glee.

"Let me introduce Charm, our newest member," Nana said, clasping her hands together. The witches hummed in approval, beckoning Charm closer.

Jade grinned as she set the cauldron in the middle of the table between a clear crystal ball and a modern record player. Beside a silver-covered dish, tarot cards were sprawled across one side of the table as though the witches had just been using them. The death card rested in the center, and Charm's heart quickened.

Nana motioned Charm to an empty spot beside her at the table. "Today is a celebration, not only for my granddaughter's birthday, but for the new life she carries inside her now. Soon enough, we'll welcome the arrival of a baby girl, who one day will join us."

Charm forced herself to smile as she placed the cloak around her shoulders and fastened it in the front.

"I'm Pamela," a woman with bright blue eyeshadow and makeup caked on her face said. "I've known about you since you were a wee thing. My beloved, like yours, is gone, but he served his purpose and gave me a beautiful daughter who you will meet next year."

Served his purpose? Was there no remorse at all? From anyone?

Charm folded her arms around her stomach, where a child would already be taking shape, if what her family had said was true. Deep down, she knew it was.

Her daughter, one day, would fall in love, then … murder her beloved. The magic thumping within her grew louder as she swallowed and half-listened to the remainder of the grim stories shared around the table. Shoved off a cliff, drowned in a lake, buried alive, died from a poisonous snake bite. Jade had run over Charm's dad, claiming it was a hit-and-run. Nana tripped her boyfriend down the stairs, said it was an accident.

Charm's stomach churned. Most of the deaths were violent, and she didn't believe it was all the amulet's doing because the witches beamed around the table, proud of what they'd done.

"Music and then a toast," Jade cheered, turning on the record player. "Cosmic Love" by Florence + The Machine filled the air, the singer's melodic voice caressing Charm's eardrums.

She tried not to let her horrified thoughts show across her expression as the women silently chanted their own words, words she didn't understand, to the music while lifting their candles, the flames igniting.

Jade nodded at Charm. It was time.

Stomach sinking, Charm picked up a candle—the amulet's magic coursed through her, traversing within her bloodstream to the tips of her fingers before lighting the wick. The power felt natural, easy.

Jade removed the lid from the silver dish, revealing a white-frosted cake. *Happy Birthday Charm* was written across its top.

She watched in her *Twilight Zone* state as Jade lit the birthday candles, just as she had for every birthday. But now Charm was surrounded by women she didn't know, a witch coven she was meant to join. A coven that asked for their pound of flesh, a price in blood.

When the song ended, Jade turned off the record player. "Make a wish."

Perspiration had gathered on Charm's palms and she rubbed them against the velvet cloak as she leaned over the cake.

Sucking in a deep breath, she blew and made the

one wish she prayed would come true.

Nana removed the lid from the cauldron, took a ladle, and poured a small amount of blood into each of the goblets. The metallic scent struck Charm's nostrils when she was served her goblet last. As she stared at the liquid softly swishing in her cup, she barely held back from heaving.

"A toast to womanhood," Nana shouted, raising her goblet high.

"To witchhood," Jade added with a grin. "Time for the celebration to begin. Now drink."

The witches brought their goblets to their lips, including Charm.

A moment later, a single, choking sound drifted through the air, echoing off the walls.

Charm's hands were shaking as the smiles on the witches' faces turned to grimaces. *One. Two. Three.* The witches fell to their knees, gasping for oxygen.

Charm set her goblet, still full, down on the table and inched back, the tempo of her breaths increasing.

"What did you do?" Jade gasped, clenching the sides of her head, her eyes becoming ivory orbs. White vines, like tattoos, snaked across her face, her arms, consuming her flesh. Charm couldn't let guilt wash over her, not now. As Charm stepped to the side, Nana reached for her leg, her hand stilling midair. Terrified screams, accompanied by the awful sound of stone rubbing against stone, filled the room as the witches fought against something they could never win. Nana's skin grew pale, frozen in place, her body turning to marble. Silence was all that remained, and as Charm took in the coven around her, all of the witches had met the same fate as her mom and Nana, their stony expressions twisted in horror.

While studying them, she knew with certainty that they were still alive, that they could hear her within their marble graves.

"My daughter," Charm rasped, gritting her teeth, "will not be a part of this. Will *not* suffer from this. And she will never know about any of this. She will not have happiness taken away from her because of my selfishness, of my thirst for power." Her gaze drifted to her mom and Nana next, their marble eyes unblinking and yet still able to see. "For what you've done, you will remain like this, *powerless*, the memories of your dark deeds spinning inside your mind forever. And that is worse than death."

The amulet around her neck lit up, heating Charm's flesh, taking, taking, *taking*. One witch's magic right after the other flowed into the jewel. Until the women were fully drained of power. The rush of what had to be dark fae magic swam through Charm's veins, coursing fast, faster. Her eyelids fluttered as she felt the power of this magic, and she *liked* it. For a moment, a part of her was tempted to leave the amulet on, see what it could do, see what *she* could do.

No! Charm wouldn't allow herself to become corrupt like the coven.

Hands shaking, she reached for the chain and let out a satisfied sigh when she unclasped it. As soon as she took the necklace off, no magic lingered inside of her. She'd sacrificed her own power to the amulet in exchange for Sage.

Her gaze fell to the women around her once more, their fearful marble faces. Tears stung her eyes as she tore the cloak from her body and let it fall to her feet. Charm then ran through the beaded curtain, up the stairs. She pushed open the door of the boulder and watched it close and seal up—no one would ever find the witches.

The amulet heated against her palm but she ignored it. She shoved it into her pocket so she wouldn't have to feel its essence. Around her, the trees murmured in the night as though they understood the emotions flowing through her, and maybe they did.

She stumbled to her car, then dropped into the driver's seat. After shutting the door, she grabbed her phone and peered at the screen.

I love you. Be careful.

Repulsion for what she had to do battled relief that Sage was alive. Relief won as she texted him back. *I love you. It's over. I'll be home soon.*

Charm hadn't thought she would be able to stop herself from murdering her true love.

Charm reached for the dagger. Brought it to Sage's throat. He froze. Peered up at her. She screamed and begged inside her head, but the amulet wasn't listening.

You want power? Isn't that what you crave, what you feed on? What if I give you the power of the coven instead? Including mine, *she pleaded, hoping that maybe the essence of the first witch was listening.*

A scream finally tore from her and she yanked her hand away from Sage's throat.

"What the hell, Charm?" Sage rasped, his eyes wide in shock. "You could've warned me you wanted to try something a bit different."

"Sage!" she cried, rolling away from him while he stared at the glowing amulet resting against her collarbone. "I need blood."

The spell had demanded Sage's blood, but if Charm had to choose between a magic that she'd never asked for or Sage, that was no choice at all. She'd pushed back tears, knowing this was not a cute and quirky witch story. It was a brutal one, and one had to be bold to survive it.

Charm took Sage's hand, slicing a diagonal line across his palm. His throat bobbed as she pinched his hand, letting the red spill from his flesh into the cauldron. She then pricked her finger and squeezed three drops of blood atop his, watching in awe as the cauldron magically filled itself to the brim with mystery blood.

"This is real," Sage whispered, wrapping a cloth around his hand.

"I told you it was." She frowned, adding the rosemary and mint to the liquid. Having made her own pact with the amulet, Charm had been allowed to confess everything to Sage.

"I know, but I was hoping it wasn't."

Charm wished it was all a nightmare too. Sage hadn't believed her at first, but he'd still been willing to let her cut his hand.

Closing her eyes, she gripped the amulet, allowing it to take her offering, her sacrifice, as was promised. The amulet warmed, growing hotter and hotter, scalding her skin. Draining her of every last drop of magic until all that she could feel was the power of the amulet itself, its thrum.

With the power of the amulet, Charm had cast a spell of her own making, to imprison one's mind, causing the potion inside the cauldron to bubble. She'd made Sage promise to stay behind, to leave town if she didn't return by midnight.

Now her hands trembled—her whole body did. The tears pricking her eyes finally fell. This was all over. No more lies. No more manipulation. No more magic at the cost of innocent lives.

She started the engine, reclined in her seat, and let her playlist blast through the speakers. As the quick beats of "Psycho Killer" thundered, she couldn't help but laugh as she cried.

She sang and sobbed along with the lyrics while leaving the forest and the coven behind. The cars might be found, but the witches wouldn't be.

When she pulled into a parking spot at her apartment, she didn't really know how she'd gotten there. Everything had been a blur while she'd zoned out and robotically driven home.

As she pushed the key into the lock, the door flew open to Sage's worried face. "I wish you had answered my text earlier than you did. I was going out of my damn mind."

"I didn't want to get distracted." Charm stepped inside, then closed the door behind her. She cradled his face and pulled him toward her. All she needed in that moment was to kiss him, and she didn't care if it was wrong or not. She would've burned down the entire world for him if it had been necessary to save his life.

Her lips pressed to his. "I swear, I won't cut your hand ever again. I mean, unless it's necessary."

"You don't have to promise me anything." He held her tight as she wept.

Charm vowed that after today, she would truly live. She would forget the horror of what she'd done, just as the witches had so easily moved past what they had done to their daughters, the terrible payments they had demanded of them, and the hearts they'd broken in the process. However, the witches wouldn't soon forget their pasts.

And her own daughter would know that true love did exist because Charm had put her and Sage first.

A soft thrum came inside her pocket where the amulet rested, purring and satisfied with Charm and its new power.

TALE TWO

ENRAPTURED

A siren's call was deadly, but that didn't make it any less beautiful.

When Auryn was a child, her mother had spun her stories about the sirens of the sea. Dazzling and alluring. Strong and vicious.

Deep in their lair, mermaids made of bone danced with corpses of their kills, selkies cuddled in the rotting flesh of those they hunted, and the sirens delighted in it all.

Don't ever go to the sea at night unless you want to die, her mother had always said. *That's when the sirens come.* But Auryn hadn't listened, not even as a child. She'd been too curious, too intrigued by how the sirens lured in their prey.

Over the years, when Auryn snuck out of her window, she would watch at the edge of the woods to see if a villager awaited their demise. Some went in hopes of the sirens ending their melancholy lives, others journeyed to see if they could get one to fall in love with them. There were many, many reasons they'd come, especially after a tale spread of a siren's ability to mend a broken heart, heal illnesses, and create immortality. But the reasons mattered not because it all ended the same for them.

In blood and death.

Auryn was twenty now, having spent her life baking in a sweltering kitchen and selling pies at her mother's market booth. Day after day, pie after pie, the same routine, over and over again. The only interesting thing that had ever occurred at her booth was when Hollis decided to come to it. Hollis, a man she had been fascinated with her entire life but had never spoken to. He'd asked her to bake him a pie she'd never made before—a challenge—and ever since that day, he had returned. Taking a piece of her heart away from the sea with each smile, each kiss. Pulling her farther from the siren's call.

Every night, Auryn sat behind her boulder and peered out at the crashing waves of the sea. Tonight, the sirens wouldn't only walk and dance across the sea—they would go to the shore to those who lingered. Near the water, in the middle of the sand, stood four young people. Three women, with their dark hair in long single braids, and a blond man wearing no tunic, his broad chest on display, spun in circles beneath the silvery moon. She didn't know what village they'd come from, nor did she recognize any of them. Yet it wouldn't have mattered even if she had because they'd chosen to come here, to listen and wait for the song of the sirens.

On this night, up high in the sky between the stars, the moon was neither a crescent nor full, not even split in half. A first quarter half-moon, like a crooked smile, gave off a glow.

The strangers' lit torches created eerie shadows that danced across the sand. The small group didn't seem to want to die on this night as they laughed and drank their bottles of wine. From their movements and their conversations, Auryn supposed they were the sort who believed they could tempt a siren, not be seduced by their song. Perhaps they wanted a tumble or thought they could retrieve a wish. Maybe this time things would be different.

But Auryn knew better.

The sea waves crashed harder against the earth, rolling across the sand and creating their own virtuous song. Auryn peered out from behind the boulder once more, waiting. For a moment, only one, she believed the villagers could be safe this evening, but she knew that was a false thought.

The blond man pressed his lips to one of the women's, and she giggled, entwining her fingers into his curls.

A light tinkling sound drifted through the air, and Auryn held her breath, her heart beating wildly in her chest, her fingers buzzing with energy. Then it started, a melody, growing louder, a song like no other, words in a language that only the sirens of the sea would know. It didn't matter that she couldn't understand what was being sung because each night she came, she imagined the lyrics that would ring true for a siren. *Come to me, be mine, let me devour you and leave only your bones.*

The villagers stopped dancing to stare toward the dark, thrashing sea. Auryn squinted, waiting for a form to come forth. And then, as though magic summoned them, four females passed through a tall wave, their steps elegant, their skin ranging from dark to pale. Wet golden hair hung to their naked waists, and they appeared human, only more perfect, not a single flaw marring them. Their eyes mirrored one another's—glowing orange irises honing in on the villagers. The song didn't cause the enchantment alone, only when their eyes locked with their prey would it work.

Auryn's heart pounded as it always did, not from fear, never from that, but something more giddy. *Anticipation.*

The humans didn't move as the sirens stepped toward them. In perfect synchronization, they lifted the strangers' chins while they sang before pressing their lips to theirs. Auryn watched in wonder, fascination, and she knew what would come next. She'd seen it happen time and time again.

First, silence came, then the strike. The sirens' movements were fast when they tore apart their prey with their sharp teeth and hands. Blood sprayed the sand, their bodies, as they ate, devoured, and all the while, the group remained enchanted, not a single scream escaping their pretty mouths.

It was a beautiful sight to behold, the same as when Auryn had been hunting and had caught wind of a bear feasting on a deer, eating its entrails. To her, the sirens' actions were natural, and the villagers were warned, just as she had been. But she'd never been a good listener, even so, she'd never let her presence be known because she wasn't that foolish. Yet a piece of her had always wanted to be a part of the sirens' family, tugging at her heart to go to the sea when the otherworldly beings were there at night, as it did in that moment.

Auryn watched the sirens lift what was left of the humans and haul them toward the sea, leaving trails of crimson in their wake. Perhaps years ago, more villagers had tried to fight the sirens, but it was rare now. No one wanted to risk being put under their spell and losing their lives to their song.

One of the sirens, who was wearing a necklace of bones, glanced back, blood dripping from her ruby lips. Her fiery gaze met Auryn's, and the female's lips tilted upward. Auryn gasped and ducked behind the boulder, waiting for her body to become theirs next, for them to sing her their song.

But when she looked back out, the sirens were gone, the only song was the whispering of the sea. A breath escaped her lips, part relieved and part disappointed.

When one of the village's own was taken, the cobbled streets were almost empty, the mood of the men and women somber. But by the end of the next day, still no one mourned the dead strangers. The market was busy as ever, and exhaustion washed over Auryn by the time she sold her last pie.

She pushed a lock of dark hair behind her ear as a figure sauntered to her booth, wearing his flirtatious smile. Her heart gave an extra thump at Hollis—his dimples, his crooked smile, the way a piece of his chestnut hair always stood up in the back. She'd never been particularly good at talking to men, but with him, it was always easy, ever since he first requested a pie from her.

"Did you save me a pie?" He grinned, leaning on the table to meet her eyes.

"What do you think?" She flicked his chest and drew out the one she'd saved from inside her booth. "I hope you like apple cinnamon."

"Mmm." Hollis grinned wider as he folded his arms behind his back, not taking the pie from her outstretched hands. "I refuse it for now." He inched closer, his warm breath mingling with hers. "How about you bring it to me tonight?"

"Why not now?" Auryn arched a brow, pressing closer to him, so close she inhaled his alluring masculine scent.

"A reason for me to get you alone." He lifted a

lock of her dark hair and twirled it around his finger.

"Hm." She set down the pie, then folded her arms and gazed into his bright blue eyes. "Will there be wine?"

"Any flavor you could want." He released her hair and backed away with his hands on his chest, a smirk on his face. "Come or you'll wound me."

She covered her mouth as she laughed, unable to stop smiling, even as he disappeared out of sight. All the village girls had wanted Hollis, but for some wonderful reason, he'd chosen her.

Auryn gathered her belongings in her wicker basket, then headed down the rocky path in the heat of summer to her cottage. Her dress clung to her body, making her wish fall would arrive sooner rather than later.

She arrived home to an empty cottage and padded to her room. Her mother was spending time with her lover in another village for the next few weeks. Auryn enjoyed the quiet. She slipped on her prettiest dress, its pale lacy sleeves falling just past her shoulders. After running a comb through her messy hair, she headed toward Hollis's with his pie.

He lived only a few cottages from her, so it barely took any time to walk the distance.

The potted daisies she'd given him greeted her on his porch. Auryn knocked and smiled when he cracked open the door with his lopsided grin.

"I didn't know if you would come," he said.

"I couldn't very well sell the pie tomorrow now, could I?" Auryn teased. She'd never given in to visiting him late at night—she'd always chosen the sea instead. But she'd met him plenty of times before darkness reigned, feeling his lips on hers, his hands trailing down her back, his fingertips digging into her waist.

A fire crackled in the corner of the sitting room, and he beckoned her with a finger to where a bottle of wine and two glasses rested on a fur rug in front of it. She sat beside him, and he poured her a glass of red wine, which they drank while sharing the pie.

"Where do you go at night?" Hollis asked, taking a deep swallow from his glass.

Auryn furrowed her brow. "What do you mean?"

"I have trouble sleeping and will go outside and stare at the stars. For years I've seen you leaving your home to go somewhere in the middle of the night."

He'd seen her? A pit formed in her stomach. They'd been together for months and had started to truly get to know one another, but he'd never once asked her about her late-night outings. "Is that why you started talking to me? To discover my secrets?"

"Yes," Hollis whispered, "I was curious, but then I fell in love with you." He drew her into his lap, her legs straddling his waist. "Is—is there another?" His voice came out unsure, worried.

Auryn wanted to laugh at the absurdity of it

because there had only ever been him … and the sirens. "No, only you." She pressed her lips to his, absorbing his warmth. "I would tell you where I go, but then you would never talk to me again."

"Nothing could make me do that." Hollis planted a soft kiss on the column of her neck, sending pleasureful tingles throughout her body. His fingers skimmed up and down her spine before caressing her hips. "Marry me."

Auryn gasped at his beautiful, unexpected words, and then her chest tightened at another thought. If he stayed an intimate part of her life, he needed to know, would have to understand her urges to go to the sea each night. She couldn't sneak away from his bed, lie, be deceitful. He deserved honesty.

Pulling back her shoulders, she sat up straight and studied his blue eyes beneath the flickering fire. "I go to the sea at night."

Hollis froze, his fingers tightening on her waist. "Do you have a death wish?"

"It's not like that." She frowned. "I don't go to be kissed, to hope for my life to be taken. I go because I like to watch them..." Watch them dance, watch them *kill*.

Hollis didn't utter a word, only stared at her as though she were mad, the look she'd never wanted to receive from anyone, especially him.

She leapt from his lap, and he grasped her wrist, but she tore away from him and bolted out the door.

His shouts echoed behind her, yet she didn't stop as she ran, not for home but toward the sea. The stars shone in the sky, flickering as if leading her in the direction of the sirens, telling her not to go home, not to run back to Hollis. *Come and watch. Come and stay*, they seemed to say.

Tears rained down Auryn's cheeks, and she wiped them away, wishing she'd never said anything to Hollis. She couldn't take back the horror on his face. Horror at what she was doing. Why couldn't she stop this madness? Why did she relish in watching people be torn apart? Villagers called the sirens monsters, but perhaps she was one herself.

Auryn ran through the forest, hopping over logs. Locusts made their clicking sounds, and a wolf howled from somewhere farther away. Chest heaving, she slowed her pace at the edge of the forest, where the sea was close. So very close.

Keeping her feet light, Auryn sank behind the boulder and peered out at the sea, where a single man with peppered hair down to his shoulders waited. He stared at the water as the waves brushed his bare feet while he held up a lantern. By the hunch of his shoulders, she believed he'd lost something, that he'd come to die.

After waiting a long while, a song floated through the breeze, its notes high and sublime, tickling Auryn's ears. Then out from the sea, a head broke the surface, the siren's golden hair clinging to her naked body as the rest of her form slipped out. It was the same siren, the one wearing the necklace of bones who had glanced at Auryn the previous night.

The man didn't move, his body frozen as he watched in wonder. Orange irises glowed from the siren, a knowing smile on her face.

She continued to sing, swaying her hips toward him. The siren stopped in front of the man and curled her long fingers around the back of his head, then pulled him toward her. The man's body relaxed when she planted her lips on his. A sigh escaped him, but the kiss didn't last long before the siren pierced his throat with her teeth, tearing it apart at the same time as she cracked open his rib cage with her bare hands. He collapsed in the siren's arms, and the female's gaze drifted to Auryn.

"I know you're there, pretty little mortal," the siren purred, blood staining her sharp teeth. "I know you've been coming for years. I know your deepest desire is to be one of us. Come tomorrow and perhaps you can be." The siren turned away then, taking her dead corpse back into the sea. Leaving Auryn alone. Breathless. Mesmerized and, for the first time, afraid.

The next day, Hollis knocked on her door, his hair

swept back, a lumpy pie in his hands.

"What is this?" Auryn arched a brow, studying the catastrophe. She didn't meet his gaze—she couldn't, not after the night before.

"I made you a pie." He stepped closer and lifted her chin with his free hand. "A peace offering."

Her lips tilted up at the edges as she finally met his kind eyes. "You don't bake."

"It probably tastes horrible, but I wanted to show you that I love you. No matter what. I still want you to be my wife." He bit his lip. "If you'll have me."

"Even with my odd habits?"

"I love your oddness." He paused, cupping her cheek. "I wouldn't ever ask you to stop anything you wished, but this is too dangerous. Please, if not for me, then for yourself. Please don't go back to the sea at night."

The way he watched her then, the hunger, the love in his eyes, Auryn would do anything in that moment for him. "All right," she finally said, bringing his face to hers and kissing him softly. "Stay? With less clothing?"

His brows rose at her unusual boldness, and Auryn laughed. She'd never been with him skin to skin, his body molded to hers, and she wanted him in every way.

"I certainly have no qualms about that," he murmured in her ear.

Auryn grabbed him by the collar of his tunic and drew him into her room. She took the pie from his hands, then set it on the nightstand. They peeled each other's clothing off until there wasn't a single barrier between them. Their kisses gradually grew from gentle to daring, their hands exploring. And then Auryn finally decided to give him the piece of herself she'd been saving. It had always been meant for him.

While they lay tangled in each other's arms, the fullness in her heart started to fade as night fell and Hollis's breaths became even. The itch to leave, to go to the sea, churned inside her as it always did. Even though she hated herself for it, she would break her promise.

"I love you." Auryn kissed Hollis once more on the lips before slipping from his warmth. She slid her dress back on and ventured out into the night.

The sea belted out its musical sounds when she arrived, but not a soul stood out on the sand, as though this night was meant just for her. Her hair whipped around her face from the heavy breeze created by the waves.

Auryn padded across the sand, her heart thrumming against her sternum. This was the first time in her life that she stood beneath the stars at the ocean's edge without her precious boulder to hide behind. If death came for her on this night, she would die fulfilled. She'd given herself to the man she loved, and now she would discover more of the sirens' world.

After waiting long into the night, when she thought the siren would never come, the female glided across the sea, walking on top of the water. Her long golden hair rested over one shoulder, and her eyes glowed a hypnotic orange, but she didn't release a song to capture Auryn, only studied her in a way a mother might a child.

The siren's voice was soft as silk as she spoke. "Come, Auryn. Come home to the sea."

She didn't hesitate and clasped the siren's cold hand. The female tugged Auryn toward the sea, the water creeping up their bodies, then to their necks, when a voice shouted from behind her, "Auryn!"

Hollis.

Auryn took a deep swallow, keeping her eyes trained on the siren. But when he shouted her name again, every emotion she ever felt for him rose within her, and she ripped her gaze away from the immortal, turning to face her beloved.

He ran toward the water, his eyes wild, his feet and chest bare. Auryn's heart lurched for him, and she wanted to stay, wanted to go back to him and be his wife, wanted to let him make another awful pie for her. She would be true to her promise this time and never come to the sea at night again.

"I don't want to go anymore," Auryn pleaded, the sound of the waves like death bells in her ears as she faced the siren. "I want to stay."

"It's too late for that now, my darling," the siren cooed, baring her razor teeth. Auryn tried to scream, but the sea swallowed her cries as she was pulled beneath the water.

Now, the skeletal remains have disappeared, along with the notebook of tales the woman once held.

If you enjoyed Savage Delights you might want to try These Vicious Thorns: Tales of the Lovey Grim!

Thorns don't always pierce the heart. But sometimes they do.

Thorna is a fae queen and has fallen for a mortal who relishes dark tales. Before she reveals her true nature to him, she hopes to win his heart by writing him stories of her own. But when the time comes for the mortal to discover what she truly is, will he accept her love or push her away?

Subscribe to Candace's Awesome Newsletter!
Join Candace's Facebook Group: Candace's Pretty Monsters

To read the first two chapters of Clouded By Envy, turn the page

CANDACE ROBINSON

CLOUDED BY ENVY

CRUEL CURSES
BOOK ONE

ONE

BRENIK
TEN YEARS AGO

Brenik could not get the vision of the headless sarillas' bodies he had seen yesterday out of his head. Their necks looked to be perfectly snapped but when he had inched closer, he could see the outline of where the skin had been ripped, blood leaking onto their dark fur. The jovkins had only eaten the heads, and the sarillas' torn bodies were left to rest in the damp grass, as if at peace.

Shaking the vision out of his thoughts, Brenik stood on a tree branch beside his sister, Brayora. He studied the creature in front of them, Junah, and listened intently to what she needed to say.

"You two must flee while you are still able— before there is nowhere for you to hide any longer," Junah said with sweat beading against her temples.

The long black horns sprouting from her forehead appeared to penetrate into Brenik's thoughts, while the shorter ones attached to her temples pointed in two different directions, as if confusing him in which way he should flee.

Brayora lunged forward and flew down to wrap her arms around Junah's thick ankle. "Junah, we do not want to run and hide away again. You have been like a mother to us this whole time, and what if something happens to Brenik? I… I would not be able to live with myself!" she cried as her tearstained face turned toward Brenik.

He wanted Bray to be free from harm, but more than anything, he wanted himself to remain safe. Turning her head back around, Bray buried her face flat against Junah's leg. Brenik watched as Bray's black braid fluttered against her obsidian wings— each thin vein seemed to pulse rapidly with the fright of having to leave their home. Bray gently lifted her head, released Junah's ankle, and took several steps back.

Brenik dove off from the branch, beating his wings until his bare feet hit the cool grass beside his sister. If not for their dark wings, sharper teeth, and pointier ears, he and Bray could easily be mistaken for fairies.

Junah's giant form knelt in front of them. She stared down at Brenik and Bray intently, her golden eyes beaming against her gray skin. Keeping silent, they waited for Junah to speak.

"I am going to let you two little ones know a secret I once attempted myself. It did not work for me, but it may for you. I did not want it to come down to this, but sometimes things do not work out the way we would like." She paused for a moment before speaking again, and worry coursed through

Brenik's small body. "Away from here—about half a day's journey to the south—you will stumble upon an ivory, rose-shaped stone. Once there, place your hand against the petals and wait for the Stone of Desire to rise, then you may ask for safe crossing. If worthy, you shall pass. If not, you will have to continue hiding. The jovkins have started to hunt the sarillas more and more, but bats are still their priority."

Brenik knew Junah was right—the fact that they were bats made them vulnerable. Their race had been long hunted in Laith by the jovkins—Junah's kind. The jovkins claimed the bats ate all their fruits, but Brenik's race was so tiny in comparison to them that it should not have mattered. But what was theirs was theirs, the jovkins seemed to think.

Reaching desperately for Bray's dry hand, Brenik clenched it with his sweat-slicked one. It irked him that she was not as frightened as him.

Pulling him closer, Bray leaned her head as far back as she could to gaze up at Junah. "I will do whatever I can to protect my brother." The tears that had streamed down Bray's cheeks were already dried, but against her pale skin, her red lips still resembled the color of blood from her sobbing.

When Brenik and Brayora were born, their mother left them behind because there were two of them. Usually, only one bat was born at a time—but there were two who drew their first breath that day.

Brenik was too insignificant for his mother to worry about, and because Bray had gotten most of the nourishment—she had been perfectly healthy. It was always her fault. Junah had found Bray and Brenik near a peach tree—instead of destroying their fragile bodies as she was meant to have done, she had taken care of them ever since.

Laying a large open hand against the luscious grass, Junah gave them both a tilt of the head. Brenik and Bray stepped forward onto her palm, and she brought them both up to her shoulder. Bray was the first to step from Junah's large hand, and she lunged for the jovkin's neck in a long hug, arms unable to even wrap halfway around her. Brenik stood on the end of Junah's shoulder and watched as she mumbled to Bray that she loved her. With one last kiss to the neck, Bray fluttered off, allowing Brenik to finally say his goodbye.

Rushing forward to the warmth of Junah's gray neck, he wrapped his thin arms around her as much as they would go—which wasn't far. "I will miss you, Junah," he said as tiny tears dribbled down his cheeks.

Junah's neck creaked as she turned to face him, and he backed away to the edge of her shoulder. She appeared tired, and her age was beginning to show—in the deep lines across her forehead and the wrinkles that sketched beside her eyes. "Brenik, there is a darkness and jealousy in you which has to stop now. I know you love your sister, but the envy needs to cease, or it will destroy everything that is a part of you. I have seen your kindness, Brenik. You both mean everything to me, so protect each other because I love you."

With a sharp inhale, he leaped from Junah's shoulder. Brenik thought about the words the jovkin had spoken and although he cared about her deeply, he could not mutter those words back.

A loud howl traveled through the forest, followed by an ear-piercing scream of agony. Brenik flinched midair because he always recognized the sound of a jovkin tearing its victim to pieces.

"Go!" Junah hissed.

Not turning back once to look at Junah, he flapped his dark wings fiercely, until he found Bray at the edge of the forest, standing on a small branch with black leaves.

"We have to hurry, little brother. It will be all right," she murmured, as if she were in charge and the only one who was okay. Well, *he* was okay, too.

Choosing not to answer his sister, Brenik zoomed right past her. *How dare she always call me little brother?* he thought. It was only because she was born before him by barely any wing beats. A trickle of laughter came from behind him as they soared through the air, like he was playing a game with her. At her sounds, a smile crossed his face because maybe he was.

Brenik's wings pumped quicker and quicker as he flew past more inky leaves. The foliage changed colors as he flew farther—to sapphire, followed by a deep pink. Hearing her inch closer, he tried to flap even faster, but she was too swift. Bray gave him a small wink when she caught up, then whipped her head forward and zipped by.

There was no sign of sweat on her face, while Brenik was soaked in perspiration. Wet beads pressed to the back of his shirt, making the material of his tunic cling heavily against his skin and slow him down.

Sighing, Brenik wanted to give up. There was nothing he was better at than her. Always second best. Always nothing. He loved her… He hated her… But he needed her because he would miss her more than anything.

"Wait, Bray!" he yelled, not wanting to be left behind by himself.

Spinning around, she gave him a playful grin until she saw his face. "What is wrong, Brenik?"

"Just… Just... Don't leave me behind. Please," he stuttered, hating himself even more for the weakness of needing her.

They both came to a halt for a moment on a large crooked branch.

"I would never leave you behind," Bray said. "I love you, and I am always here to protect you. Always have been—always will be." She wrapped her arms tightly around his back, and tugged him into a solid hug.

Pausing for a moment with his hands at his sides, Brenik finally brought them up to hold her just as tight. She was his only family now. When they were first born, right before they could fly, Bray had attempted with all her might to carry him because he was not strong enough to move his wings. She helped him get through it, yet it was also her fault that he was the way he was—even though it was not.

Brenik pushed the conflicting thoughts away. "I am here for you, too," he said. They had only been alive in Laith for ten years, but after all they had been through, it felt much longer than that.

Slowly releasing him, Bray dove from the tree. Before he followed, Brenik scanned the ground below and his eyes widened with fright. Bones had been thrown and scattered across the lush greensward that was now splattered in blood. The jovkins must have torn the bodies apart, ate what they wanted, and disposed of the bones like they were nothing.

Brenik didn't want to worry Bray, so he leaped off the gnarled branch and trailed near her to search for the Stone of Desire. He kept his thoughts away from Junah and what lay ahead, because it would have to be better than the death that awaited them if they remained in Laith.

Together they flew and they flew, through the

blend of trees that were all a blur except the leaves' embodiment of color that warped Brenik's vision. Time had no meaning until the sound of water flowing awoke him from his trance. Slowly, Brenik let his wings lessen their movement right as Brayora did the same.

A large white boulder slid into view. "Brayora, look! I think that is it," he called.

His sister's head twisted back to him, then whipped around to where he was frantically pointing. "You are right, little brother. That has to be it."

Higher and higher Brenik flew, until he could tell the structure on top of the stone was the shape of a rose. The rock was bright white and dark shadows danced around it under the twin suns' specks of light. Already, they were in the process of setting to make room for the twin moons to rise.

Closer. He needed to draw closer. Swishing his wings back and forth, slower and slower, he let his body descend toward the top of the rock's creases before landing in between two folds. Shortly after, Brayora dwindled down beside him.

Kneeling on the rough stone, Brenik lifted his hand to press it to the grain at the same time as Bray whispered, "Put your hand against it like Junah said."

"I know," he shot back, scowling. She did not need to remind him how to do everything. Her expression told him she was sorry, yet she still monitored his movements closely.

Brenik smacked his hand against the boulder while his sister gently pressed down on it. Shifting his focus from the rock to Bray's face, Brenik found no answer of what was to come. Her gaze penetrated the rock as if she was trying to command it to move—but everything was *not* commanded by her like she thought it was.

At that precise moment, a hard quake knocked Brenik backward. He struck the right side of his wing against the rough edge of the rock fold. *Maybe she does command everything.* He rubbed the tip of his wing where it throbbed, then hopped off the Stone. Bray repeated his motions and lingered close beside him.

His hands rested by his sides, fingers fluttering with nervousness, when another vibration from the Stone shook the ground. Dirt surrounding the white rose rock slithered away in broken fragments.

Bray appeared to be the epitome of calm, while Brenik wanted to fly back to Junah to let her know what had occurred. His heart pounded and ached at having to leave Junah. But no matter what, he could not go back. The jovkins could already be making their way to where Junah was.

The large rock ascended from the ground as a consistent convulsion shook the surrounding trees. Birds rapidly chirped above them, then stormed away, causing a few crunchy brown leaves to rain down upon Brenik.

Bray and Brenik floated to the ground. The jolting noises stopped after the rock had grown into something new, almost oval-like. It stayed perfectly still, unmoving. Then it happened. It awakened, unfolding from different areas: long, thin legs emerged from the bottom—alabaster stone arms appeared from the sides. A head poked forward like a turtle coming out of its shell, and the rose structure seemed to glide downward to cover its back.

At the sight of the Stone's head, Brenik took two steps back. Shaking, Brenik gritted his teeth and bit the side of his tongue to make it bleed, so he could focus on something else. The two eyelids of the Stone leisurely opened to reveal eyes the color of raven wings. No nose. No mouth. But somehow it spoke in a voice that was low and deep.

"What do you desire?" The voice didn't come from outside, it came directly inside Brenik's head.

Bray's lips parted, seeming startled, too. Neither one of them said anything to each other, both only focused on the creature in front of them.

"What do you desire?" the voice boomed inside Brenik's skull once again. Burning flames seemed to lick inside his head. He lifted his hands and placed them against his temples to try and make the stinging sensation stop.

Bray, ever the brave one, spoke up for the both

of them. "A jovkin named Junah sent us here and said you may be able to send us away—somewhere safe."

Tilting its head to the sky, then gingerly angling it down, the Stone crawled toward them. "So, you want me to save you. Why should I do this?"

"Please, I want you to help my brother. Harbor us, but most of all protect him." Bray fell to her knees in pleading.

"And you?" The Stone's head shifted lower until it was just a hair's breadth from Brenik's face.

"Yes, please save me. I—I won't be able to survive if you leave me here."

"What about your sister?"

"Yes," he rushed the words out. "Her, too." He did not want to be separated from his sister on the journey, and he would not leave without her.

Suddenly, the Stone shuffled backward. Brenik thought the Stone would leave them both there, but then it spoke, "I will grant access, but only because of her—how badly she wants to save you. She is pure and will be granted a gift to survive where I will be sending the both of you. If you agree, you may pass."

Brenik did not understand why Bray was to be granted a gift and not him. His shoulders slumped, and his heart sank because this was how it always was and always would be. Again, he was only second best. But for their escape, he would agree to anything. "We agree," he murmured.

The Stone of Desire nodded and slid a hand across the dirt, flipping its palm upward for them. Brenik stepped onto the stone with his bare feet pressed against the roughness, while Bray flew down toward the middle, grabbing his hand.

Brenik's body quivered as the arm coasted backward, afraid they were going to be eaten. But since the creature had no mouth, he was not sure how that would be possible. They were pulled under and farther back into the depths of shadows, until there was a flash of white light, followed by another bout of darkness.

TWO

BRAY
PRESENT DAY, 1995

Bray tossed the note against the tree wall and let out a frustrated sigh. He left again. The drawing from the letter played over in her head: a basic sketch of their tree, and Brenik flying away from it. That meant he would be gone for a while.

Should I be so desperate for him to stay? Just because I want him to? she thought. Brenik was her brother, and he should be able to go off whenever he wanted. But she was so alone here. *Ruth.* Bray couldn't think about her either. Ruth was gone—had been gone for a year.

This world was supposed to be so much better than Laith and for a time, it was, until it wasn't. Brenik had been distant since Ruth died, and now Bray was completely alone. She lay back down on her silky yellow hammock and tilted her head up toward the roof of the tree, staring at the words she and Brenik had carved in the ceiling over the years. Their first word was *Junah*, so they would always remember her, and the next was *Laith*, to remind them where they had come from. The last word they carved was *Ruth* because she had given them everything. Brenik would always stand close by as Bray carved each word with care.

No new words since then.

A shuffling sound ripped Bray from her torturous thoughts. It sounded like Ruth was in her garden, but she reminded herself that Ruth would *never* plant any bushes or flowers again.

More stirring—the sound of digging—spread through the tree. Bray leaped from the hammock and crept to the edge of the hole to peer out, just as she heard a loud grunt. A shovel struck the ground, and two filthy hands held the tool in his sweaty grip. No shirt, a headful of brown hair that fell past his earlobes, and no face. Well, he did have a face, but Bray couldn't see it yet.

Quietly, Bray pulled her small body from the edge and tightened her dark wings against her back, prepared to flee.

Though she was practically on her stomach, Bray lifted her head back up to peep out of the hole to get a better look. Natural brown skin reflected the sun's rays, and the guy was lean with well-defined muscle—but not to the point where it was ridiculous.

Turning away from Mystery Face, Bray discovered he had a whole garden waiting to be planted: white roses, yellow daisies, and green bushes. She had no idea what the last ones really were, so she would just call them green bushes. Ruth had a beautiful garden once, until everything died, along with her.

"Hey, I'm heading to school now. I'll see you after," a voice called from farther away. Bray's gaze automatically turned to the back of the house where a small boy—who must have been about seven—stood. Bray wasn't very good at guessing ages, so maybe he was six. She wasn't sure. His haircut looked like a bowl sitting on the top of his head with the hair parted and split smoothly down the center. It wasn't as bad as some of the hairstyles she had seen when she used to watch TV with Ruth and Brenik, though. The boy's baggy striped shirt fell to his knees, almost the same length as his shorts, hiding the remainder of his thin upper arms and legs.

"Okay, Lu. Do you want me to drive you today?" Mystery Face twisted his neck to look over his shoulder at the little kid. Not a mystery anymore. His face was nice, matching the kid's younger one. *Might be about twenty-five, possibly had the kid a little young*, she decided.

"No, I like the walk." The kid smiled wildly and shifted the backpack on his shoulder.

Nice Face set down the shovel and walked closer to the kid. "You sure, Luca? I'm about to head off to work, and it's on the way."

"I got this. I gotta learn to take care of myself."

Nice Face's expression turned into not such a nice face. "Someone bothering you at school?"

"No, just gotta impress." The boy's—who Nice Face had called Luca—wild smile became a bit tamer and practically said there was no bullying to worry about.

"O—kay," Nice Face said almost skeptically, studying the kid for a few extra seconds. His tight shoulders seemed to relax a fraction. "Well, I'll be home around four, so see you then. Love you."

"Love you, too." Luca pivoted on his heels and gave Nice Face a tilt of the head goodbye.

Nice Face picked the shovel back up off the ground and resumed his digging. Bray wondered where the mom was—probably already at work. Ruth's house had been sitting there for a long time with a for sale sign in the front yard until about a month ago. Bray guessed the new family was finally there and must have moved in the day before.

Growing bored of watching the guy dig holes, Bray crawled away from the open space and stood. She crashed down on the hammock, letting it sway her back and forth. *What is on the list of things for me to do today?* she wondered. *Oh, that's right, my usual— sleep.* If Brenik was there, they would probably just sit in silence—at least that was better than being completely alone.

Bray wasn't sure how long she had drifted off for,

but a puddle of wetness rested against her cheek when she woke up. *Okay, so it's only drool from myself.* Lifting a hand up toward her cheek, she swiped the saliva away and rubbed it on to the hammock. *Classy,* she thought, but there was already some gathered there anyway.

Remembering the events from earlier, Bray headed straight to the hole and peeked out. She shifted her head from left to right. *Nothing.* Bray looked up and down, noticing a few bushes had already been planted in the dirt.

Then she saw it: a circular stone bowl filled with water sitting on top of a long thick stem, attached to a circular bottom. *A birdbath!* With a huge grin, Bray stepped on the ledge of the hole and leaped off, flapping her wings hurriedly to the nearest pink and yellow peach. Opening her jaw wide, she bit into the thin skin. *A juicy one.* The fruit filled her mouth with delicious pleasure, and she took one more long bite before diving down to the birdbath.

The top of her newfound treasure was a perfect circle with tiny mounds around it resembling hills. Bray landed on the ceramic and bent down to take a seat, before placing her bare feet into the warm water that had been thoroughly heated from the gleaming sun.

Peering down at the clear water, Bray saw no sign of intrusion from other creatures yet. She rotated her head in every direction, as if she would be caught just by thinking about slipping into the water—still no sign of life.

Flicking her braid over her shoulder, Bray pursed her lips together to hide the smile shining against her face and jumped into the water. The splash echoed. Her bare feet scraped the rough bottom, while her dress inflated and then clung to her body as she shot to the surface. She let out a small giggle to herself. It was sad that the only highlight of the past year was hopping into a shallow pool of water with no one around except for her.

She leaned back into the liquid, floating and moving her arms slowly up and down, while swimming in figure-eight circles.

Bray closed her eyes and let the water cover her ears, so that nothing in the world existed, except for the muffled vibrations from the liquid.

A loud boom startled Bray out of her daydreams and her eyes flew open to meet two dark irises, warm brown skin, and that black bowl hair.

Tiny human.

Luca.

Freeze, Bray thought to herself, not even blinking her eyes. She held them wide open, thinking he wouldn't notice her, or maybe he would just assume she was a bird. Even though he was staring at her and had spoken something she didn't hear clearly.

Nope. That isn't going to work. He hovered closer, his eyes scrunched halfway closed to examine her more thoroughly. Unable to hold her lids open any longer, Bray blinked several times.

"What are you?" he asked, genuine amazement creeping into his words, his lips slightly parted.

"A bat!" Bray yelled, and she jumped up from the warmth of the water, darting straight for the tree hole.

Chest heaving, Bray landed inside and collided with the floor. She rolled to her back, running both hands down her face. "Why did I come out without paying attention? I know not to!" Ruth had always told her this.

A quake trembled through the tree, causing shivers to run up and down her spine. *What is the little beast doing? Oh no, what if he's trying to chop down the tree? My home—the peaches!* Bray didn't know why she was thinking about stupid peaches when there was another fruit tree directly next door.

Despite the thunderous rumbling, Bray grabbed the needle from underneath her hammock and dodged toward the window. If the little beast thought he could take her down, then he had another thing coming. She would prick his eye— actually, she would poke both of his eyes to protect her and Brenik's home.

When Bray reached the edge of the window, the sound stopped. She peeped her head out of the hole, right as a face met hers, his black hair falling forward over a hazel eye—an eye she was going to poke.

Startled, she jumped back instead of toward him.

A broad smile crossed the little beast's face. "Hello."

Freezing once again, until she remembered that the staying-still-as-a-statue strategy didn't work in the birdbath, she meekly said, "Hi."

Bray brought the needle up toward his smiling face, just in case.

"Are you planning on sewing something?" He tilted his head at the needle.

"Yeah, your eyeball." She gave him a hard glare.

"What?" he asked while laughing hysterically.

He was laughing? Not scared? Bray brought the needle closer. "You need to leave and never come back. This is *my* home."

"No. Technically, it's my brother's home," he said, still smiling.

"What brother? You mean your dad who was planting out there this morning?"

Luca shook his head, and she didn't miss the wince before he spoke. "No, that's my brother, Wes. I don't have a mom or dad."

Stomach sinking, Bray lowered the needle. "Oh. Me neither. I only have a brother, but he will be gone for a while." She paused and glanced at the note Brenik had left behind, her chest tightening. Then she shrugged it off and shifted her gaze back to the boy. "By the way, my name is Brayora, but you can call me Bray." For some reason, she wasn't worried anymore about the human.

"I'm Luca Duran." He plopped his thin fingers on the edge of the hole.

"Yeah, I heard your name this morning, little beast. I mean, Luca." She thought little beast suited him better than Luca.

"Little beast?" He grinned.

"Sorry, I thought you were trying to tear down the tree." Softly, she lifted his fingers from the ledge of the hole.

"Um, I don't think I could do that without an ax. I'm not *that* strong." He seemed strong enough to her, even though he was much smaller than his brother.

"How old are you anyway? Six?"

Pulling his head back from the tree, Luca straightened his neck and narrowed his eyes. "What? I just turned ten and am in the fifth grade," he said proudly.

"Six… Ten… Same difference." Human children his age all appeared the same to her.

Luca cocked his head, as if trying to look older than he was. "No, six is a baby. I'm no baby."

"You can keep on thinking that." Bray laughed and set the needle back on the floor.

"How old are you?"

Bray tugged her shoulders back. "I'm twenty."

"So you're old then, like my brother. He's twenty-three."

Scowling, Bray placed her hands on her hips and took a step toward him. "What? I'm not old!"

"My mom was nineteen when she had Wes, so it would definitely make you old."

Bray wasn't sure how old her mother was when she had her and Brenik.

"I'm going to ignore that statement," she huffed.

"Well, see ya." Luca started heading down the tree, limb by limb.

"Wait! That's it?" Bray dove out, flapping her wings, and halting in front of Luca's face as his feet struck the ground.

"I need to eat a snack. I'm starving and just got home from school." He brushed a few beads of perspiration away from his forehead.

Her stomach growled at the word *snack*, and it was loud enough for Luca to hear.

He hiked his thumb back at the door. "Do you want to come in?"

"No. I don't want to be seen," she said half-heartedly. It was enough for one person to see her today, but it also felt good to have someone to talk to. Her gaze kept training on the door, and Luca didn't miss it.

"Wes isn't home yet—and don't worry, I won't tell him." He held his hand up in front of her face and crossed his index and middle finger.

One tiny human who seemed trustworthy enough shouldn't be a problem. Bray plopped down on Luca's shoulder like they had known each other for an eternity, and he walked inside the house—Ruth's house.

Except it looked nothing like her home anymore and hadn't in a very long time. After it was cleared out, Bray never went back inside. Now, there were cardboard boxes sprawled across the large living room. Against the wall was a floral couch, and diagonal from it rested two blue sitting chairs. A large box TV was propped in the center of the room, pushed up to the opposite wall. Bray ached to turn it on because it had been so long since she had used one.

Luca took out two blueberry muffins from the tiny pantry in the kitchen, padded into the living room, and set the wrappers on a rectangular wooden coffee table across from the sofa.

Flipping on the television, Luca shuffled to the VHS tapes and popped one in that was already halfway through the movie. He swiveled back around and opened the muffin wrapper for Bray. She landed on the coffee table and focused on eating the blueberry part first.

"So you're a fairy, like from *Peter Pan*?" Luca asked, while he stuffed most of the muffin into his mouth, letting small crumbs fall into his lap.

"No, I'm a bat." Bray angled her head in the direction of the TV and pointed furiously at the furry creature with big ears on the screen. "Hey, we have those in Laith."

"A Mogwai?" Luca's eyes bulged with excitement.

"What? No, a drogwai." She had no idea what a Mogwai was, but that creature on the screen looked incredibly similar to a drogwai.

"Okay, well, Gizmo is a Mogwai," Luca corrected.

"That is incorrect."

"I'll take your word for it, since you say you're a *bat* and all," he said with sarcasm lacing each word, and a big smile spreading, showing a row of crooked bottom teeth.

Bray's lips tugged to the side, and she opened her mouth to speak when a car door slammed shut outside. Her chest tightened, making it difficult to breathe. She had to get out of there.

"Crap, Wes is home. Hurry!" Luca sprinted for the back door, tearing it open, and gesturing for Bray to escape. She zoomed out without a proper goodbye and pumped her wings as hard as she could toward the tree hole, until her body slammed against the floor.

Hurriedly, while still out of breath, Bray gazed out the hole and saw Luca giving her a thumbs up from the glass window before heading back to his brother.

Also From Candace Robinson!

Wicked Souls Duology
Vault of Glass
Bride of Glass

Marked by Magic
The Bone Valley
Merciless Stars

Cruel Curses Trilogy
Clouded By Envy
Veiled By Desire
Shadowed By Despair

Faeries of Oz Series
Lion (Short Story Prequel)
Tin
Crow
Ozma
Tik-Tok

Cursed Hearts Duology
Lyrics & Curses
Music & Mirrors

Immortal Letters Duology
Dearest Clementine: Dark and Romantic
Monstrous Tales
Dearest Dorin: A Romantic Ghostly Tale

Campfire Fantasy Tales Series
Lullaby of Flames
A Layer Hidden
The Celebration Game
Mirror, Mirror

**These Vicious Thorns: Tales of the Lovely
Grim**
Between the Quiet
Hearts Are Like Balloons
Bacon Pie
Avocado Bliss

Vampires in Wonderland Series
Rav (Short Story Prequel)
Maddie
Chess
Knave

Demons of Frosteria
Slaying the Frost King
Frost Mate
Frost Claim

Once Upon A Wicked Villain
Spindle of Sin

Acknowledgments

Writing these things is hard for me because I never know exactly what to say even though there is so much I wish I could get out. But from the bottom of my heart, thank you for coming on this journey with me to read these short dark tales! There's always something soothing to me about writing short stories. I just love them so much.

An ear-piercing shot to my readers who are freaking amazing! I also want to thank SiriGuruDev and Carla for helping me develop these and to Amber H., Elle, and Jerica for finetuning them! To Katya, Narelle, and Julie for bringing these to fruition!

And last, sometimes we just need a little dark in their stories. Or at least I do!

About the Author

Candace Robinson spends her days consumed by words and hoping to one day find her own DeLorean time machine. Her life consists of avoiding migraines, admiring Bonsai trees, watching classic movies, and living with her husband and daughter in Texas—where it can be forty degrees one day and eighty the next.

9 781960 949257